CW00502344

Beau and Benji

The first book from a currently undefined series of books from author, Kelly Partridge.

Beau
and
Benji

Benji lay sprawled across the bed.

"This is the life," he thought to himself, while being stroked lovingly by his parent.

"I sure am the King of this Castle," he purred.

As a young grey and white tabby kitten, he had spent almost a year of his life living in the wild, after being abandoned by his first owner, until those lovely people rescued him.

They brought him to a massive place with lots of cats just like him.

It was ok, but he wasn't used to being stuck in the one place, with lots of humans peering in at him all the time.

He was happy when he was adopted
by his family, and for thirteen years
he had lived like a king.

He'd had a couple of hairy moments over the years, but he was younger then and a bit of a rascal.

One of the worst days he had was when his parent's mummy and daddy brought their big clumsy Labrador with them on a visit.

Benji wasn't going to have that big furry beast in his domain. No way. He made sure he sent him packing.

Now he spent lazy days lounging around and getting lots of cuddles. He might try to catch a bird every now and then, if he wanted some excitement or could be bothered, but he couldn't run around stalking them all day like he used to.

He heard his
family leave the
house and after
a big stretch,
he sauntered
down the stairs
to get a snack.

Afterwards, he decided it was far too much effort to go back upstairs and so he casually meandered over to the sofa to catch another forty winks.

He woke to an empty house. "They've been gone a while," he thought to himself.

He was just about to venture outside when he heard his family at the front door. He jumped off the sofa and made his way coolly to the hallway to greet them.

They came in and he noticed that they were walking slowly and speaking to him in the same strange high-pitched tone that usually meant he was going to go out in the car.

He was just about to run and hide, when the youngest one crouched down to cuddle him.

The grown up gently crouched down too and as he did, two sleepy brown eyes peered out, and a furry head popped up from behind his arm.

Benji studied the intruder carefully. He didn't know what to make of him.

"And just what on earth are you supposed to be?" he demanded.

"Where am I?" The voice that replied was squeaky and quiet. The Cavalier King Charles Spaniel puppy's wide eyes were exploring the room.

"You're in my house." Benji declared, growing more irritated. "You had better state your business. Where did you come from?" he commanded. "How did you get here?"

"Umm, I don't know," the squeaky voice replied. "I was in a big thing that moved for a really long time, and now here I am."

"Hmm, must have been the vets," Benji thought.
"Or maybe grandma's house." Suddenly the
intruder began walking gingerly around his house.
"The cheek of it!" Benji thought.

"How dare he!" He watched him vigilantly.
"If he takes any of my food, he's going to be
in big trouble." Benji thought crossly.

Benji saw that his parent was putting down bowls of food and water on the other side of the kitchen. She was gesturing to the invader to have some. "Good job," Benji thought.

He watched as the creature cautiously sniffed around the food and water bowls before deciding he wasn't going to take part.

"Umm no. No thank you.
I don't trust it."
The small furry pest said.

Benji he knew he needed to be careful. He didn't want to get into trouble by making his feelings known about this trespasser too early.

He huffed, turned around and sulked off upstairs.

"You can stay one night," said Benji as he marched off.

"And you had better not be here when I wake up in the morning."

Beau
and
Benji

Beau and Benji.©

Printed in Great Britain
by Amazon

61175021R00015